Dora and Diego's ADVENTURES!

SIMON SPOTLIGHT/NICK JR.
New York London Toronto Sydney

Based on the TV series *Dora the Explorer*® as seen on Nick Jr.®

SIMON SPOTLIGHT
An imprint of Simon & Schuster Children's Publishing Division
1230 Avenue of the Americas, New York, New York 10020

Manufactered in the United States of America
First Edition
2 4 6 8 10 9 7 5 3 1
ISBN-13: 978-1-4169-3532-2
ISBN-10: 1-4169-3532-0
These titles were previously published individually by Simon Spotlight.

Contents

Meet
Diego!

adapted by Leslie Valdes
based on the original teleplay by Eric Weiner
illustrated by Susan Hall

¡Hola! I'm Dora, and this is my friend, Boots. We're at the Animal Rescue Center, where they help all kinds of animals.

Eeep, eeep!

Errr, errr!

I hear a sound. Look—Baby Bear is about to fall out of the tree! Hang on, Baby Bear! Oh, no—he's falling!

Here comes my cousin, Diego. He's saving Baby Bear. Wow! Diego's really cool. He can make animal noises and talk to wild animals.

Can you say "Errrr, errrr!" to Baby Bear?

Uh-oh! Someone's calling for help. Diego's field journal helps him identify animals. Let's check it to figure out who's calling for help.

It's Baby Jaguar, and he's in trouble! We've got to get to the waterfall to help him!

Map says that to get to Baby Jaguar we need to go through the rain forest and past the cave, and that's how we'll get to the waterfall. Will you help us save Baby Jaguar? We have to hurry! *¡Vámonos!*

We made it to the rain forest! Look—there's a zip cord! We can ride the zip cord through the treetops and zip through the rain forest.

Do *you* see a ladder we can climb up?
Oh, no! The ladder is missing six rungs. Let's find the rungs.

Thanks for helping fix the ladder. Now let's go save Baby Jaguar. Wheee!

Meow, meow!

We made it to the cave! Do you see a polar bear?

Diego's journal says polar bears live only in the cold. But it's really, really hot in the rain forest. . . .

Oh, no! That's not a polar bear! Do you know who it is? It's Swiper, that sneaky fox. He'll try to swipe Diego's journal. We have to say "Swiper, no swiping!" Say it with me: "Swiper, no swiping!"

Thanks for helping us stop Swiper! Now we need to find the waterfall. We can use Diego's spotting scope to see things that are far away!

There's the waterfall. . . . And there's Baby Jaguar!
We're coming, Baby Jaguar!

We can water-ski down the river to save Baby Jaguar. Diego says if we ask the dolphin, he'll pull us through the water. Can you help me call the dolphin? Say "Click, click!" Again!

Click, click!

The dolphin can pull us through the river, but we need something to hold on to. Let's check Backpack! Say "Backpack!" What can the dolphin use to pull us along the water?

A rope! *¡Excelente!* We all need to hold on to the rope. Put your hands out in front of you and hold on tight. Whoaaaa!

Yeah! We made it to the other side of the river.

Oh, no! Baby Jaguar is about to fall over the giant waterfall! Diego says the big condors can help us: They can fly us all the way to Baby Jaguar. Say "Squawk, squawk!" to call the big condors!

Squawk, squawk!

Quick! You have to help us fly to Baby Jaguar! Flap your arms. Faster!

Meow!

Hooray! We caught him!

We saved Baby Jaguar, and now the whole Jaguar family is together again. Thanks for helping!

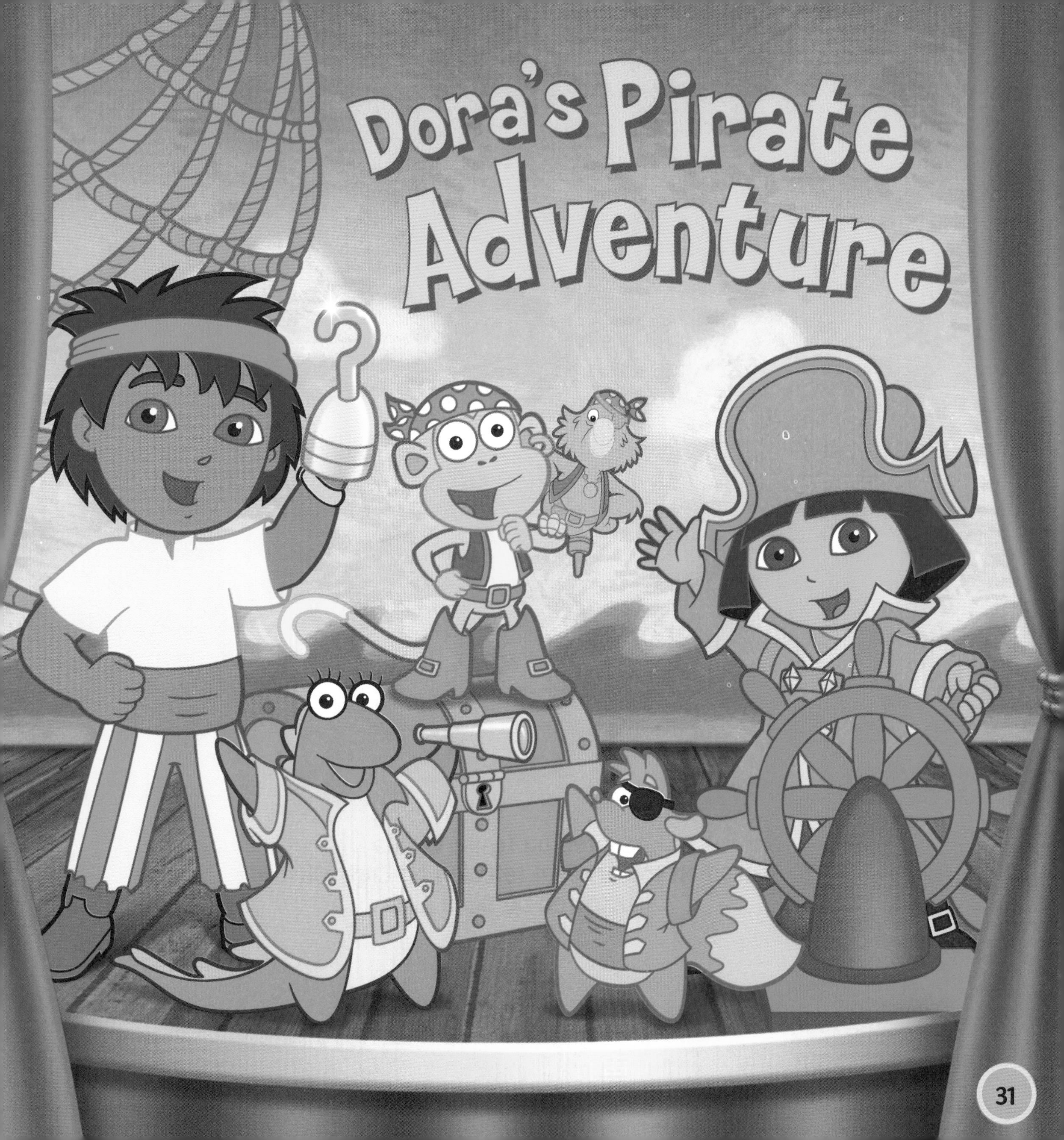
Dora's Pirate
Adventure

adapted by Leslie Valdes
based on the original teleplay by Chris Gifford
illustrated by Dave Aikins

Ahoy, mateys! I'm Dora. Do you want to be in our pirate play? Great! Let's go put on our costumes!

Uh-oh. That sounds like pirates. Do you see pirates?

The Pirate Piggies are taking our costume chest! They think it's full of treasure.

If we don't get the costumes back, we can't dress up like pirates. And if we can't dress up like pirates, then we can't put on our pirate play.

We can get our costumes back. We just have to know where to go. Who do we ask for help when we don't know where to go? The Map!

Map says the Pirate Piggies took the treasure chest to Treasure Island. We have to sail across the Seven Seas and go under the Singing Bridge, and that's how we'll get to Treasure Island.

Do you see the Seven Seas? Yeah, there they are! We can use that boat to sail across!

¡Fantástico! Now it's time to sail the Seven Seas. Let's count the Seven Seas together. *Uno, dos, tres, cuatro, cinco, seis, siete.*

Good counting!

Now we need to find the Singing Bridge. Where is the bridge?

Yeah, there it is. *¡Vámonos!*

The Singing Bridge sings silly songs.

Row, row, row your boat,
Gently down the stream,
Merrily, merrily,
merrily, merrily,
Life is but a
bowl of spaghetti!

We have to teach him the right words.
Let's sing the song the right way.

Row, row, row your boat,
Gently down the stream,
Merrily, merrily, merrily, merrily,
Life is but a dream!

Yay! We made it past the Singing Bridge! Next up is Treasure Island. Do you see Treasure Island? Yeah, there it is!

Look! There's a waterfall. Isa has to turn the wheel, or we'll go over the edge.

Uh-oh! The wheel broke! Maybe Backpack has something that will help us. Quick, say "Backpack!"

We need something to fix the wheel. Do you see the sticky tape?

Yeah, there it is! *¡Muy bien!*

Turn the wheel, Isa!
Whew! We made it past the waterfall.
Come on! Let's go to Treasure Island, and get our costumes back!

We found Treasure Island. Now let's look for the treasure chest. We can use Diego's spotting scope.

There it is! Come on, mateys, let's go get our costumes back!

The Pirate Piggies say they won't give us back our treasure. We need your help. When I count to three, you need to say "Give us back our treasure!" Ready? One, two, three: Give us back our treasure!

It worked! *¡Muy bien!* The Pirate Piggies say we can have our treasure chest back!

Thanks for helping us get our costumes back. Now we can put on our pirate play. We did it! Hooray!

Dora's Big Dig

by Alison Inches
illustrated by Robert Roper

¡Hola! I'm Dora, and today I'm digging in the garden. *Dig! Dig! Dig!*

Wow! I uncovered a turquoise stone. Ooooh, maybe this is an ancient treasure!

I should take this stone to my *mami*. My *mami* is an archeologist. That means she digs for ancient treasure! She'll know what to do with an ancient treasure.

First I need to pick up my friend Boots.

Look, Boots! The stone has a jaguar's face carved into it, and the jaguar is wearing a crown.

Boots and I are going to need *your* help to get to the pyramid to see my *mami*. Who do we ask for help when we don't know which way to go? Yeah, the Map! Say "Map!"

Map says that we have to go across Emerald Canyon. Then we have to climb down the Steep Steps, and that's how we'll get to my *mami.*

¡Vámonos! Let's go!

Do you see Emerald Canyon? There it is! But it's so deep! How are we going to get across? Do you see something we can use to zip over the canyon?

Yeah! We can use the zip cord!

Wheeeeee!

We made it over Emerald Canyon!

Uh-oh! Do you see Swiper? I think that sneaky fox wants to swipe our turquoise stone. We have to stop him. Quick! Say "Swiper, no swiping!"

Thanks for helping us stop Swiper. Where do we go next? That's right—the Steep Steps!

Do you see the Steep Steps? There they are!

Wow, these steps are really steep! Let's hold on to the rail.

We have to climb down ten steps. Will you help us count?
¡Uno, dos, tres, cuatro, cinco, seis, siete, ocho, nueve, diez!

We made it down the Steep Steps! Good counting! And there's my *mami* at the pyramid.

Mami! Mami! Look what I found!

Mami says the stone belongs at the Museum of Ancient Art. We can take it there right away. *¡Vámonos!* Let's go!

The museum director says we found an ancient treasure—the missing piece from the stone jaguar's medallion!

We can put the stone back where it belongs.

We did it! We found and returned the stone. *¡Gracias!* Thanks for helping!